# IRREVOCABLE

## STUDY GUIDE

# STUDY GUIDE
# IRREVOCABLE

Joe Phillips

ARROWS & STONES

# CONTENTS

# STUDY 1

# THE CALLING

## (CHAPTERS 1-3, 5-8)

What are some examples of an existential crisis? Have you ever experienced this? Explain your answer.

_____

_____

_____

_____

_____

_____

_____

_____

_____

_____

What are some biblical examples of an existential crisis?

_____

_____

_____

_____

_____

_____

_____

_____

What do you think John Mark Wright is going through?

_____

_____

_____

_____

_____

_____

_____

_____

What is "calling"? This word can have so many meanings both in the religious and secular communities. Is it what God's drawing you to or is it just something you "feel" drawn to? Does it mean going out to the mission field in a far-off land or can it be as simple as fulfilling that childhood dream of becoming a mom (or dad)? In the end, either one of those can be the call on your life—the purpose you were made for. When you find your calling, it becomes a core part of you and what you give to the world. Once you find and follow God's calling on your life (just like when you accept Christ as your Savior or get married), it doesn't mean that the road is easy. Following God's call on your life takes work and sacrifice. Are you up for following God's calling?

_____

_____

_____

_____

_____

_____

_____

_____

_____

What does a "calling" mean to you?

_____

_____

_____

_____

_____

_____

_____

_____

Have you ever felt called to something? What was it?

_____

_____

_____

_____

_____

_____

_____

_____

What's your calling? If you don't know, take some time now to explore what it might be.

_____

_____

_____

_____

_____

_____

_____

Do you know anybody like the golfer in chapter one? Who? Why do they remind you of the golfer?

_____

_____

_____

_____

_____

_____

_____

_____

In your own words, what is a Pentecostal handshake? Have you ever received one of these?

_____

_____

_____

_____

_____

_____

_____

Why did John Mark's calling upset the grandpa in chapter three?

_____

_____

_____

_____

_____

_____

_____

Has anyone ever gotten upset (or jealous of) your calling?
Who? When?

_____

_____

_____

_____

_____

_____

_____

_____

What did John Mark Wright have going for him? Explain.

_____

_____

_____

_____

_____

_____

_____

_____

What do you have going for you? Explain your answer.

_____

_____

_____

_____

_____

_____

_____

_____

_____

> *In relation to the gospel they are enemies on your account, but in relation to God's choice they are beloved on account of the fathers; for the gifts and the calling of God are irrevocable. For just as you once were disobedient to God, but now have been shown mercy because of their disobedience, so these also now have been disobedient, that because of the mercy shown to you they also may now be shown mercy.*
>
> ROMANS 11:28-31

## QUESTIONS ABOUT THE PREVIOUS SCRIPTURE:

Have you ever been summoned to a meeting that you knew nothing about? How did this make you feel?

_____

_____

_____

_____

_____

_____

Why might John Mark Wright become nauseous at the opportunity presented to him in chapter five?

_____

_____

_____

_____

_____

_____

Has a seemingly good opportunity that has come your way ever made you feel uneasy? Explain the situation.

_____

_____

_____

_____

_____

_____

_____

_____

*For where jealousy and selfish ambition exist, there is disorder and every evil thing. But the wisdom from above is first pure, then peace-loving, gentle, reasonable, full of mercy and good fruits, impartial, free of hypocrisy.*

JAMES 3:16-17

## QUESTIONS ABOUT THE PREVIOUS SCRIPTURE:

Have you ever harbored selfish ambition when being a part of a team? Have you ever experienced someone else on your team with this trait? What are the dangers of this?

_____

_____

_____

_____

_____

_____

_____

How do you think John Mark Wright felt in chapter seven? Would you respond the same way?

_____

_____

_____

_____

_____

_____

What stood out to you about the interview in chapter eight?

_____

_____

_____

_____

_____

_____

_____

_____

Are you open to change? What in your life are you never willing to change and why?

_____

_____

_____

_____

_____

_____

_____

_____

In your own words, describe the "immutable and unchanging nature of God."

_____

_____

_____

_____

_____

_____

_____

_____

_____

# STUDY 2

# THE MISSILES

## (CHAPTERS 9, 15-17, 21-27, 37-41)

At what point did Bill step out of line with his infatuation?

_____

_____

_____

_____

_____

_____

_____

_____

_____

What "missiles" are you struggling with in your life?

_____

_____

_____

_____

_____

_____

_____

_____

What are "the missiles"? The missiles are representative of the sinful desires, obstacles, difficulties, and uncertainties we face as we pursue God's calling on our lives. Missiles will always be present if what we are pursuing is worthwhile—don't let their presence deter you from doing what you know to be right. What missiles are you struggling with today?

How would you describe the demeanor of the interim bishop in chapter 15?

_____

_____

_____

_____

_____

_____

_____

_____

_____

_____

Do you think you would be able to work for the interim bishop? Have you ever worked for or with someone similar? Describe the experience.

_____

_____

_____

_____

_____

_____

_____

_____

_____

What was lost in chapter 17?

_____

_____

_____

_____

_____

_____

_____

_____

How are the two churches in this chapter different? Are they similar in any way?

_____

_____

_____

_____

_____

_____

_____

_____

Describe John Mark's emotions in chapter 21. Have you ever felt this way?

_____

_____

_____

_____

_____

_____

_____

What is your most embarrassing moment? How did it make you feel—besides embarrassed?

_____

_____

_____

_____

_____

_____

_____

Describe John Mark and Layla's confrontation. Would you have acted similar to John Mark?

_____

_____

_____

_____

_____

_____

*Now the scribes and the Pharisees brought a woman caught in the act of adultery, and after placing her in the center of the courtyard, they said to Him, "Teacher, this woman has been caught in the very act of committing adultery. Now in the Law, Moses commanded us to stone such women; what then do You say?" Now they were saying this to test Him, so that they might have grounds for accusing Him. But Jesus stooped down and with His finger wrote on the ground. When they persisted in asking Him, He straightened up and said to them, "He who is without sin among you, let him be the first to throw a stone at her." And again He stooped down and wrote on the ground. Now when they heard this, they began leaving, one by one, beginning with the older ones, and He was left alone, and the woman where she was, in the center of the courtyard. And straightening up, Jesus said to her, "Woman, where are they? Did no one condemn you?" She said, "No one, Lord." And Jesus said, "I do not condemn you, either. Go. From now on do not sin any longer."*

JOHN 8:3-11

## QUESTIONS ABOUT THE PREVIOUS SCRIPTURE:

What stands out to you about how Jesus handled this situation?

_____

_____

_____

_____

_____

_____

_____

_____

What did the Pharisees do wrong in this passage?

_____

_____

_____

_____

_____

_____

_____

What does this passage reveal about John Mark's situation?

_____

_____

_____

_____

_____

_____

_____

_____

Why do you think the radio soured John's day in chapter 37?

_____

_____

_____

_____

_____

_____

_____

_____

Would the radio issue have rattled you if you were in John Mark's shoes?

_____

_____

_____

_____

_____

_____

_____

Have you ever struggled with addiction? Describe the experience. Where are you at now with this struggle?

_____

_____

_____

_____

_____

_____

_____

_____

Have you ever been as lonely as John Mark was? What did you learn in that season?

_____

_____

_____

_____

_____

_____

_____

_____

> *The LORD gave this message to Jonah son of Amittai: "Get up and go to the great city of Nineveh. Announce my judgment against it because I have seen how wicked its people are." But Jonah got up and went in the opposite direction to get away from the LORD. He went down to the port of Joppa, where he found a ship leaving for Tarshish. He bought a ticket and went on board, hoping to escape from the LORD by sailing to Tarshish.*
>
> JONAH 1:1-3

## QUESTIONS ABOUT THE PREVIOUS SCRIPTURE:

Why do you think Jonah chose to not follow God's commands?

_____

_____

_____

_____

_____

_____

_____

Have you ever tried to run from your divine calling? What was the result?

_____

_____

_____

_____

_____

_____

_____

How does John Mark's story relate to Jonah's?

_____

_____

_____

_____

_____

_____

_____

_____

_____

What is the significance of the stump in chapter 27?

_____

_____

_____

_____

_____

_____

_____

_____

_____

In what way does the gun represent fits of rage?

_____

_____

_____

_____

_____

_____

_____

_____

_____

What is the brown Bible on the stump representative of?

_____

_____

_____

_____

_____

_____

_____

_____

_____

# STUDY 3

# THE PEOPLE

## (CHAPTERS 4, 11-14, 18-20, 28, 30-31, 36, 42-43)

How would you define "church hurt"? Have you ever experienced this?

_____

_____

_____

_____

_____

_____

_____

Has your current church or a past church you have attended ever had conflict? What was it about?

_____

_____

_____

_____

_____

_____

_____

Have you ever been "ambushed" by someone you loved or trusted? How did this make you feel? Were you able to forgive them?

_____

_____

_____

_____

_____

_____

_____

_____

_____

What are "the people"? The people section of this study is about the men and women God places into our lives at exactly the right time. Whether it's an old friend who has an encouraging word or a random encounter that provides wisdom, God knows exactly who we need and when we need them. Who are the people God has placed in your life?

Why could John Mark trust the bishop in chapter 14?

_____

_____

_____

_____

_____

_____

_____

_____

Who do you have in your life that you can trust and go to for advice?

_____

_____

_____

_____

_____

_____

_____

_____

Explain the tumor metaphor told to John Mark by the bishop in chapter 14.

_____

_____

_____

_____

_____

_____

_____

In what ways is "unoffendability" a superpower? Are you unoffendable?

_____

_____

_____

_____

_____

_____

_____

_____

What is the significance of the change from John Mark to John?

_____

_____

_____

_____

_____

_____

Have you ever lived without direction? Where does your direction come from now?

_____

_____

_____

_____

_____

_____

_____

_____

_____

*Bear one another's burdens, and thereby
fulfill the law of Christ.*

GALATIANS 6:2

## QUESTIONS ABOUT THE PREVIOUS SCRIPTURE:

Who do you have in your life that can share your burden?

_____

_____

_____

_____

_____

_____

_____

What burdens have you shared in the past with others?

_____

_____

_____

_____

_____

_____

_____

_____

Who is sharing John Mark's burden? List all that apply.

_____

_____

_____

_____

_____

_____

_____

_____

> *Then He poured water into the basin, and began washing the disciples' feet and wiping them with the towel which He had tied around Himself. So He came to Simon Peter. He said to Him, "Lord, You are washing my feet?" Jesus answered and said to him, "What I am doing, you do not realize right now, but you will understand later."*
>
> JOHN 13:5-7

## QUESTIONS ABOUT THE PREVIOUS SCRIPTURE:

What is the significance of Jesus doing this for His disciples?

_____

_____

_____

_____

_____

_____

_____

_____

_____

In what way can you emulate Jesus in this passage in your daily life?

_____

_____

_____

_____

_____

_____

_____

_____

How does this passage relate to the people in John Mark's life?

_____

_____

_____

_____

_____

_____

_____

_____

What does the flat tire at the end of chapter 42 represent?

_____

_____

_____

_____

_____

_____

_____

_____

_____

_____

_____

_____

# STUDY 4

# THE RESTORATION

## (CHAPTERS 10, 29, 32-35, 44-51)

What do you think led to the church revival in chapter 10?

_____

_____

_____

_____

_____

_____

_____

_____

How has God restored you in your past?

_____

_____

_____

_____

_____

_____

_____

_____

> What is "restoration"? This study covers the act of restoration by God despite the bad that has occurred. No matter where you've been or what you have been through, God has the ability to restore—it is our responsibility to go to Him for this restoration. What is holding you back from restoration?

What does the phrase "It was what was invisible that made him apprehensive" in chapter 44 mean?

_____

_____

_____

_____

_____

_____

_____

_____

How is the fact that our gifts and callings are irrevocable demonstrated in chapter 44?

_____

_____

_____

_____

_____

_____

_____

_____

What do you think about the altar call in this chapter?

_____

_____

_____

_____

_____

_____

_____

_____

Do you feel it is necessary to die to self before you can be restored? Why or why not?

_____

_____

_____

_____

_____

_____

_____

_____

How does Chapter 47 demonstrate the differences in the styles of the two Bishops?

_____

_____

_____

_____

_____

_____

_____

How would you describe the atmosphere of the room in chapter 50? Have you ever experienced an environment like this?

_____

_____

_____

_____

_____

_____

_____

_____

How do you think being "weathered by life" changes ministry?

_____

_____

_____

_____

_____

_____

_____

_____

> *And the son said to him, 'Father, I have sinned against heaven and in your sight; I am no longer worthy to be called your son.' But the father said to his slaves, 'Quickly bring out the best robe and put it on him, and put a ring on his finger and sandals on his feet; and bring the fattened calf, slaughter it, and let's eat and celebrate; for this son of mine was dead and has come to life again; he was lost and has been found.' And they began to celebrate.*
>
> LUKE 15:21-24

## QUESTIONS ABOUT THE PREVIOUS SCRIPTURE:

What does this passage reveal about God's love for us and
His restoration?

_____

_____

_____

_____

_____

_____

Based on this passage, is it ever too late to be restored by God?

_____

_____

_____

_____

_____

_____

*And through you have not seen Him, you love Him, and though you do not see Him now, but believe in Him, you greatly rejoice with joy inexpressible and full of glory, obtaining as the outcome of your faith, the salvation of your souls.*

1 PETER 1:8-9

## QUESTIONS ABOUT THE PREVIOUS SCRIPTURE:

What does this passage mean?

_____

_____

_____

_____

_____

_____

_____

_____

_____

What does this scripture reveal about our joy?

_____

_____

_____

_____

_____

_____

_____

_____

How does this scripture relate to John Mark's restoration?

_____

_____

_____

_____

_____

_____

_____

_____

What does the pulpit represent?

_____

_____

_____

_____

_____

_____

_____

_____

What is the significance of the radio? What does this represent?

_____

_____

_____

_____

_____

_____

_____

_____

_____

What do you think the glass of whiskey and the Hennessy bottle represent in this story?

_____

_____

_____

_____

_____

_____

_____

_____

What do the four items John Mark had in front of himself (Cognac, legal pad, gun, pen) represent?

_____

_____

_____

_____

_____

_____

_____

What does John Marks' mother's obituary signify?

_____

_____

_____

_____

_____

_____

_____

What do you believe is the significance of the tear-stained altar
in chapter 45?

_____

_____

_____

_____

_____

_____

_____

_____

What is the significance of The Rolling Stones poster in chapter 47?

_____

_____

_____

_____

_____

_____

_____

_____

What does the basin represent?

_____

_____

_____

_____

_____

_____

_____

_____

www.ingramcontent.com/pod-product-compliance
Lightning Source LLC
Chambersburg PA
CBHW072357020726
47506CB00004B/1157